Happy 2nd Birthday
to our precious
Sam.

Lots of love,

Auntie Catherine,
Uncle Jim, Jaimie,
Lauren & Rachel
xoxoxoxoxo

BIRDS

BIRDS

By Kevin Henkes

Illustrated by Laura Dronzek

Greenwillow Books

An Imprint of HarperCollinsPublishers

Birds. Text copyright © 2009 by Kevin Henkes. Illustrations copyright © 2009 by Laura Dronzek. All rights reserved. Manufactured in China. www.harpercollinschildrens.com. Acrylic paints were used to prepare the full-color art. The text type is Goudy Modern. Library of Congress Cataloging-in-Publication Data. Henkes, Kevin. Birds / by Kevin Henkes ; illustrated by Laura Dronzek. p. cm. "Greenwillow Books." Summary: Fascinated by the colors, shapes, sounds, and movements of the many different birds she sees through her window, a little girl is happy to discover that she and they have something in common. ISBN: 978-0-06-136304-7 (trade bdg.) ISBN: 978-0-06-136305-4 (lib. bdg.) [I. Birds—Fiction.] I. Dronzek, Laura, ill. II. Title. PZ7.H389Bg 2009 [E]—dc22 2007045084 First Edition 10 9 8 7 6 5 4 3 2 1 Greenwillow Books

For our parents and our children

In the morning,

I hear birds singing through the open window.

Birds can be **yellow**

or **blue**

or **brown**

or **red,**

or even **green**, I think.

Sometimes they are so **black** that you can't see

their eyes or their feathers, just their shapes.

Birds
can be
BIG

or

little

or any size in between.

Once I saw seven birds on the telephone wire.

They didn't move

and they didn't move

and they didn't move.

I looked away for just a second . . .

and they were gone.

If birds made marks with their
tail feathers when they flew,

think what the sky would look like.

If clouds were birds,
the sky would look like this.

Or this.

Sometimes, in winter,
a bird in a tree
looks like one red
leaf left over.

If there are

lots of birds

in one tree

and they all

fly away

at the

same time,

it looks like

the tree

yelled,

If I were a bird, I'd ask where
all the other birds go

when it's stormy and they can't
get home to their nests.

I like to pretend I'm a bird.

I can't *really* fly,

but I can do this . . .

I can sing!